NAUGHTY STORIES

Compiled by Barbara Ireson
Illustrated by Tony Ross

HUTCHINSON
London Sydney Auckland Johannesburg

First published in Great Britain in 1989 by
Hutchinson Children's Books
An imprint of Century Hutchinson Ltd
Brookmount House, 62–65 Chandos Place,
Covent Garden, London WC2N 4NW

Century Hutchinson Australia (Pty) Ltd
88–91 Albion Street, Surry Hills, NSW 2010

Century Hutchinson New Zealand Limited
32–34 View Road, Bergvlei 2012, South Africa

Set in Baskerville by Deltatype, Ellesmere Port

Printed and bound in Great Britain by
Mackays of Chatham PLC, Chatham, Kent

British Library Cataloguing in Publication Data

Naughty stories
1. Children's stories in English,
1945–. Anthologies
I. Ireson, Barabara
823′.01′089282 [J]

ISBN 0–09–173893–8

Contents

The Boy Who Made Faces

Eileen Colwell

There was once a boy called Fred. He was not at all a nice little boy. He left his toys out in the rain, he hated washing, he pulled the cat's tail, he drew on the wallpaper, he said 'Shan't' when anyone asked him to do things.

One day he found out that he could make such ugly faces that it upset everyone who saw them. Soon he gave up his other tricks and just made faces instead. Only to look at him gave little girls bad dreams and when his friends played with him and were winning he would make such horrible faces that they were put off and lost the games. 'It's not fair!' they said and they wouldn't play with him any more. When Fred's favourite aunt came to see him he pulled such a frightful face that she never came back again but just sent a card on his birthday. The only person who didn't see him making faces was his mother – he didn't want to upset *her*. So she was surprised when

1

visitors screamed or fainted because of the horrible faces Fred was making behind her back. 'Freddie is such a kind little boy,' she said, 'and he always has a nice smile.'

Fred wouldn't listen to his friends and relations when they warned him that his face would stay that horrid shape if the wind changed. 'Pooh!' said Fred rudely, and stood out in the wind when it was changing to see what happened. But nothing did.

His father smacked him but that only made him twist his face more because it had hurt. At school he spent a lot of time in the corner looking at the wall so that the teacher couldn't see the faces he was making. She said it made her forget what she was supposed to be teaching – not that the children minded that.

It didn't matter what people said or did, Fred made faces and that was that.

One day Fred's Uncle Charles came to see him. He had been in faraway foreign countries for years and years and this was the first visit since Fred was born. Fred was very excited about his uncle's visit for he would bring a present of course – all proper aunts and uncles do – and he might know some different kinds of faces Fred could make, the kind they make in Peru or Timbuktu.

Uncle Charles did bring a present, a carved wooden monkey, which Fred thought was rather dull. Uncle Charles looked quite ordinary any-way except that he carried a walking stick everywhere and sometimes pointed it at people who annoyed him. When he did so the stick lighted up at the end with a blue crackly light and the people stopped whatever they were saying and went away very quickly. Otherwise nobody worried for they thought it was probably the odd way people behaved in the foreign countries where Uncle Charles had been living.

Sometimes, too, Uncle Charles would put his hand in his pocket and bring out some strange creature, a jerboa or a salamander perhaps. 'Oh well,' said Fred's mother, 'Charles was always interested in Nature.' Perhaps so, but Fred wondered why the salamanders and other creatures were all colours of the rainbow and why they suddenly vanished. Sometimes Fred would ask his uncle why he carried these strange

creatures in his pockets and where they went
when they disappeared. 'Strange creatures in my
pockets? Rubbish, boy!' said Uncle Charles. 'You
can see for yourself there are none there.' And he
turned his pockets inside out.

At first Fred didn't make faces at Uncle
Charles because he was too interested to see what
his uncle would do next and, besides, he was a
little nervous of him. But one day he forgot and
made a frightful face. Uncle Charles watched him

with interest. 'Not bad,' he said kindly. 'Do it again.' Fred did. 'Hmm. . . .' said Uncle Charles thoughtfully.

'Would you like to enter for a competition in making faces? You might do well.'

'Oh, could I?' asked Fred, delighted. 'Where is the competition?'

'There's a fair in the town,' said Uncle Charles. 'There should be one there. Let's go, boy.'

So off they went together, Uncle Charles carrying his walking stick as usual. 'How nice to see Freddie and his uncle such good friends,' said Fred's mother.

At the fair there were all sorts of things to see – a Fat Woman, performing dogs, a very large man who could lift heavy weights marked ONE TON. There were hot-dog stalls and candy-floss stalls and several kinds of roundabouts. Fred chose to ride on one which had cars and aeroplanes, but Uncle Charles preferred a jungle roundabout and rode on a lion, his long legs dangling on either side. Fred *thought* he heard the lion roar and saw it shake its mane when Uncle Charles got on its back, but he must have been mistaken, of course.

Several times when they had to pay for seeing things or riding on things, Uncle Charles put his hand in his pocket and brought out one of the strange creatures. Fred had to remind his uncle that they wouldn't do instead of money. 'Dear me, where could those have come from?' said Uncle Charles as the salamanders and jerboas disappeared. The people at the fair watched in astonishment.

Fred wasn't very good at throwing the wooden balls at the coconut shy, but however badly he threw, he was surprised to find that he nearly always hit the coconuts. Then he noticed that when Uncle Charles pointed his stick at the balls, they turned round in the air and hit the coconuts with a bang. Fred collected a whole armful of them and the man in charge didn't like it at all. 'Clear off, guv'nor,' he said crossly. 'It ain't fair!'

So Uncle Charles gave him all the coconuts back except one for Fred to take home.

Then they came to a large tent which had a poster outside – COMPETITIONS. TRY YOUR LUCK. Fred and his uncle paid their money and went in. In a dark corner sat an old man with a rubbery kind of face. He was saying in a tired, hoarse voice, 'Make faces and win a bicycle!' over and over again.

'Ha! Now's your chance, boy,' said Uncle Charles.

Fred went up to the old man and so did three other children. 'Wot you does,' said the old man, 'is to stand on this 'ere platform and make as many different horrid faces as you can, see. The one that makes the most faces and keeps it up longest wins the bicycle.'

The first boy was so nervous that, instead of making horrid faces, he looked quite pleasant and gave up almost at once. The next entrant, a girl, did so well that the old man told her to wait. The third to enter was Fred.

'Now, Fred, do your best. Don't let me down,' said Uncle Charles.

Fred began. He made face after face while Uncle Charles looked on approvingly.

Fred went on, changing expressions as fast as he could. At first he enjoyed it, but soon his face began to get tired. 'Isn't that enough?' he asked, but the old man didn't answer but only stared at him with his mouth open like a fish.

'Keep it up, boy,' said Uncle Charles, clapping loudly.

Now Fred was making such horrible faces and so fast that he even frightened himself when he caught sight of his face in the mirror on the canvas walls.

'Can't I stop now?' he asked imploringly.

'Don't you want to win?' said his uncle. 'Come, come, get on with it.'

On and on went Fred until his face ached all over. 'Do let me stop!' he begged.

'Faster, *faster*, FASTER!' said his uncle relentlessly – and Fred burst into tears. 'I can't bear it any longer,' he sobbed.

'STOP!' exclaimed Uncle Charles and he pointed his stick at Fred and the old man. A blue light crackled and Fred found himself at his uncle's side. His face had stopped moving and it felt stiff all over.

'Next!' said the old man hoarsely.

'I want to go home,' said Fred, sniffing.

'But you might win the prize! The other boy may not do as well as you did.'

'I don't care what he does,' said Fred. 'Let's go

home *please.*'

'Better luck next time,' said Uncle Charles. 'You'll improve with practice.'

'I don't want to practise. I don't want to make faces ever again,' said Fred.

Next morning Uncle Charles had gone before Fred woke up. Fred still felt he didn't want to make faces. He went to school and the teacher didn't put him in the corner once and the other boys seemed quite friendly, although Fred couldn't think why they had changed.

One morning Fred looked in the mirror and saw a boy he didn't recognize, a boy with a cheerful expression and a nice, friendly smile. It was himself! And behind him he saw Uncle Charles; and his uncle was smiling too. The next moment there was no one there. How could there be!

A few days afterwards, a large packing case arrived addressed to Fred. Inside was a marvellous bicycle with all the extra gadgets Fred had longed for. The carved wooden monkey Uncle Charles had given him made a splendid mascot for the handlebars.

'Now, whoever could have sent this to you, darling?' asked his mother. Fred was sure it was Uncle Charles but he never said so to anyone for, after all, Uncle Charles was in a faraway country and couldn't possibly know that Fred had stopped making faces. Or could he, perhaps?

Isabelle the Itch

Constance C. Greene

When she got home, Isabelle stomped out to the kitchen. It was empty so she stomped upstairs. Her mother was looking at herself in the mirror critically.

'They say lines lend character to a face,' she said moodily. 'If that's true, I must have some character.'

'Why can't I have a pyjama party tonight?' Isabelle whined.

'Because your father and I are going to a party, that's why.'

'So what?' Isabelle sprawled on her mother's bed, messing up the bed-spread. 'We could take care of ourselves.'

Her mother looked at her. 'Some days I'm too old to be a mother and today's one of them.'

'Some days you look too old and some days you look too young,' Isabelle told her. 'This is one of your old days.'

'Thanks, that makes me feel a lot better.' Isabelle's mother got a long dress out of her wardrobe and held it up against herself. 'They say if you never throw anything out, eventually it'll come back into fashion,' she said. 'Wasn't I smart to hang on to this?'

'Who's baby-sitting?' Isabelle grumbled.

Her mother put blue stuff on her eyelids and drew a mouth over her own with a new lipstick. 'Mrs Oliver has a virus so I guess Philip will have to be in charge. We're only going a couple of blocks away and I'll leave the number.'

Isabelle hurled herself on the floor and kicked at the rug. 'I won't stay with him,' she stormed. 'He's a big boss when he's in charge. He bosses me around something terrible. I'll run away.'

She stomped into her room and started throwing things around. She threw her favourite copy of the *Wizard of Oz* into a corner, then she opened her wardrobe door and threw her shoes

and rubber boots out and started cleaning the wardrobe floor with her shirt-tail.

'I bet the neighbours would be shocked if they saw the dirt in this house. That wardrobe hasn't been cleaned in a month of Sunday's,' she said at the top of her voice.

Isabelle's mother was sensitive about her house cleaning. She wasn't too good at it. Nothing drove her crazy faster than people who said they just didn't know what was the matter, but they couldn't stand a less-than-immaculate house. Isabelle's mother always said there were lots more important things in this world than a kitchen floor you can eat off.

When she ran out of nasty things to say, Isabelle went to the kitchen and stuck her finger into the jar of peanut butter as far as it would go.

ISABELLE WAS HERE, she wrote in peanut butter on the fridge door.

Her father stood in the doorway.

'Get a sponge and wipe that off,' he directed.

Isabelle scrubbed off the peanut butter while he watched. For good measure, she scrubbed out the kitchen sink. Hard, as hard as she could, she scrubbed until it shone.

Her father inspected her work.

'When you set your mind to it, you can do a first-class job,' he told her. He put his hand on the top of her head, something he did only when he was pleased with her. Isabelle stood very still, enjoying the warm weight of it.

'I'll tell you one thing, Isabelle. When you make up your mind to do something, you can do it. Someday you're going to scale mountains,' he said softly. 'When you stop trying to beat the world single-handed, things will fall into place for you.' He hugged her. She smelled the scent of his clothes with delight and thought he was right.

'Mum said I can't have a pyjama party,' she said.

'Is that one of those affairs where you don't close your eyes all night?' he asked.

Her mother twirled in front of them, showing off her dress and dangly earrings.

'You going some place?' her father asked.

'The Gwynnes. I told you last week.'

'Look how I cleaned the sink for you, Mum,' Isabelle said.

'Terrific. It hasn't looked that clean for weeks.'

'I don't want to go to the Gwynnes,' Isabelle's father said. 'They bore me.'

'You get to have all the fun,' Isabelle went upstairs and looked up Mary Eliza's number.

'Shook residence, Mary Eliza speaking,' a voice said.

'Let me speak to Mary Eliza Shook please,' Isabelle said.

Silence. 'This *is* Mary Eliza,' the voice said in an irritated way.

Isabelle made a very loud, very rude noise into the receiver and hung up.

She went back to the kitchen.

'You have a choice.' Her mother took two TV dinners out of the freezer. 'Salisbury steak or meat loaf.'

'You'd better tell Philip not to hit me,' Isabelle said. 'The last time you left him in charge, he ate all the ice cream, plus a jar of apple sauce, and he put his feet on the couch. *And* he said I had to go to bed at nine but he stayed up until he heard the car coming.'

'How do you know?' her mother asked.

'I spied on him. He called up his friends and swore at them over the telephone too.'

'Maybe I'd better stay home to see that law and order prevails,' her father said.

'What if I get a pain in my stomach or a

14

toothache? Philip wouldn't know what to do and I might even die.' Isabelle could feel the tears start.

'I'll speak to him before we go,' her father said.

Isabelle went to her room and threw a few more things around until she heard Philip come home.

'What do you want?' she said, going down to the kitchen and taking the two TV dinners out of the freezer.

'I'll take the Salisbury steak,' he said.

'No you won't. I want it. Mum said I get first choice.'

'That's OK, monster, you made me lose my appetite anyway,' he said.

After her parents had left for the party, Isabelle put on her swimming mask and flippers and filled the bath with water so hot that it left a red mark on her as far as it reached. She lay face down in the water looking at the bottom of the bath. No man-eating fish there. She kicked as hard as she could, escaping from the mysterious blue whale. When she surfaced, she was gratified to see the amount of water covering the bathroom floor. The ends of her fingers were puckered. She wouldn't have to take another bath for a month, she was so clean.

Isabelle put on her dressing gown and pyjamas and ate her Salisbury steak. It was tough. The peas and carrots tasted green and orange. The mashed potatoes didn't taste at all. She threw half

the dinner away, then went upstairs to get a sock out of her drawer. Placing it over the telephone receiver to disguise her voice, she made another telephone call.

'Hello,' a man's voice answered at Sally Smith's house.

'This is Sgt Brown down at the police station,' Isabelle said through the sock. 'We have complaints that you're making too much noise at your house. We might have to send a squad car over if you don't stop all the yelling.'

She hung up and made hideous faces at herself in the mirror.

PHILIP IS A FINK, she wrote in huge letters on her blackboard. Wet hair streaming on either side of her face, she lay down on her bed and, before she could stop herself, fell asleep.

Trouble with the Fiend

Sheila Lavelle

It takes some doing to play a trick on the whole class at the same time, but Angela managed to think of a way. And of course once again it was me that got the blame.

She worked herself up in a right old temper that day, and it was only because everybody laughed at her during the art lesson. Angela hates art anyway, and Miss March is always telling her off for messy, untidy work.

It was an interesting sort of lesson, because for a change we weren't doing painting. We were learning how to do that old-fashioned italic writing. And we all had those special pens with thick nibs and little bottles of black Indian ink.

We had to copy a poem from the blackboard, and I was quite enjoying making the nice curved shapes of the letters and putting fancy squiggly bits on the capitals. I only made one or two small blots, and on the whole I thought my effort wasn't too bad.

Angela, in the desk behind mine, wasn't getting on at all well. Everybody was working away quietly, with Miss March walking around the class looking over our shoulders and helping here and there, so we could all hear Angela sighing and moaning and screwing up her sheet of paper to start again.

'This is murder,' she hissed in my ear. 'This lousy pen doesn't work. It keeps making blobs.'

'Try a new nib,' I whispered, starting on the last line of the verse.

Angela clattered out to the front of the class to change her nib from the box on the shelf. When she got back to her place with a fresh piece of paper she found Miss March looming over her like a mountain.

'Angela Mitchell,' said Miss March grimly. 'I can't believe you haven't even started yet. Your paper's still blank. What have you been doing all this time?'

'She's been writing blank verse, Miss,' said that cleverclogs Laurence Parker. 'Like Shakespeare.' And you should have heard the groans from the rest of the class.

'You've only got five minutes left, Angela,' went on Miss March coldly, ignoring Laurence's remark. 'If it's not finished by the end of the lesson you'll have to stay in after lunch. Now please get on with it.'

I hoped Miss March might say something nice about my work on the way past, but she only gave it a quick glance and a nod and walked on. I finished the poem and put a neat little row of dots at the bottom. I blotted the ink carefully with a clean piece of blotting paper, then I looked over my shoulder at Angela.

She was scribbling away like a maniac, her face all red and her fingers smudged with ink. Her paper was a mess, all covered in splashes and dribbles and blotches, and she kept jabbing the pen furiously into the ink bottle as if she was trying to stab it to death.

The bell went for lunch and Angela finished just in time. She slumped back in her seat and flung down the pen with a huge sigh.

Miss March came to have a look. She picked up Angela's paper and glared at it in silence for a while. Angela didn't even look at her. She sank down in her chair, her eyes fixed on the desk.

'A five-year-old could have done better than this,' said Miss March finally in a grim sort of voice. 'It looks as if ten drunken spiders fell in the ink and crawled all over the page.' And of course that's when the whole class fell about laughing. Not because it was all that funny, but because it was a teacher's joke.

Laurence Parker got the job of collecting all the

papers and everybody else trooped out down the corridor.

'Never mind,' I said to Angela, giving her arm a squeeze. 'At least Miss Quick March didn't keep you in.' Angela was hardly listening. She had a very funny look in her eyes.

'They didn't have to laugh at me like that,' she said moodily. 'I'll think of a way to get even with the whole stupid lot of them. You'll see.'

And all the time we were eating our school dinner in the dining hall Angela sat like a statue staring into space. She hardly ate any of her stew and carrots and mashed potatoes, or her apple crumble and custard, much to the delight of Laurence Parker, who scoffed the lot.

When we were on our way out into the playground after lunch Angela grabbed me by the arm.

'Charlie,' she said, and my heart sank when I saw the gleeful expression on her face. 'I've had a fabulous idea.'

She dragged me along the corridor towards the changing rooms at the end. There was nobody around at this hour as they were all outside. Angela shoved me down on the bench beside the girls' lockers and sat beside me.

'What's first lesson this afternoon?' she said, making her eyes go all narrow.

'Games,' I said at once. 'It's Tuesday, isn't it? It's games all afternoon.'

'Right,' said Angela. 'And what will happen if we take half an hour to get changed?'

'Miss March will do her nut,' I said. 'She only gives us sixty seconds, and then she blows that stupid whistle.' I looked into Angela's face, hoping for some sort of a clue. 'What are you up to?' I said.

Angela gave me a quick hug. 'You and me, Charlie, are going to cause chaos this afternoon. We're going to mix up all the games kits, so that everybody ends up with the wrong shorts and T-shirts and stuff. Can you imagine what it'll be like? It'll be a right old shambles.'

I could imagine it very clearly and I was horrified at the thought. I stood up quickly and started to argue. But Angela pushed me down again firmly.

'You're not going to say you won't help me, are you?' she said, hands on hips. 'Because if you are I'm never going to be your friend again. So you can make up your mind, Charlie Ellis.' And she started pulling shorts and T-shirts and plimsolls out of people's lockers and muddling them up in a heap on the floor.

And do you know, for once in my life it didn't take long for me to make up my mind. I sat there thinking about all the things she had ever done to get me in trouble, and all the nasty tricks she'd played on me in the past and I found it wasn't

22

such a horrid decision, after all. I was better off without her, if only I could find the courage to tell her so.

I jumped up in a hurry before I had time to change my mind. I took a deep breath and looked her straight in the eyes.

'Well I think it's a stupid idea and it'll just cause trouble for everybody and Miss March will get mad and she's sure to keep us in until she finds out who did it and for once it's not going to be me that gets the blame because this time you can do your own dirty work. So there.'

Angela's mouth dropped open and she was giving me a real frosty-nosed stare.

'All right,' she said. 'If that's the way you want it. But you'll be sorry, Miss Hoity-toity Ellis. Don't say I didn't warn you.'

Angela started rummaging round in the lockers again and I scuttled off down the corridor as fast as I could to the playground, feeling relieved at my escape. And when I got outside I found that nice new girl Nicola Daley sitting all by herself on the wall in the sunshine. She's tall and skinny like me and she's got lovely long shiny brown hair and she's going to be a dancer when she grows up. Anyway, she gave me such a nice big smile when she saw me that I went over and sat beside her.

'Where did you live before you moved here?' I said, to start the conversation.

'Yewesly,' she told me, with a giggle. 'It's near Manchester. Funny name for a place, isn't it?'

'Not half,' I agreed. 'There was a young lady from Yewesly. . . .' But I had to stop there because I couldn't think of a rhyme.

'Who always would breakfast on muesli,' said Nicola. And we both burst out laughing.

So we sat there on the wall giggling away like anything together and making up a funny poem to send in my next letter to Uncle Barrie, and the last line was so awful I knew my Uncle Barrie would love it.

There was a young lady from Yewesly,
Who always would breakfast on muesli.
When asked for her diet,
She said 'You should try it,
It's muesli, in Yewesly, usually.'

By the time the bell went we were the best of friends, and we were enjoying ourselves so much that I'd forgotton all about Angela and her latest plot. It was only when Miss March blew her whistle in the corridor that I remembered, and my stomach suddenly rolled over as if it was full of live eels.

'You have sixty seconds to change, starting from NOW!' bellowed Miss March, and everybody rushed to their lockers and started pulling out their games kit.

'Hey, this isn't my T-shirt,' somebody called out.

'I've got the wrong shorts,' squealed somebody else.

Everybody started shrieking and yelling and fighting and snatching things from one another and chucking plimsolls around and in no time at all it was absolute pandemonium. I looked for Angela and there she was, right in the middle of the fun, giggling helplessly and shouting 'Who's got my bloomin' T-shirt?' at the top of her voice.

Well, some of them didn't half look daft, I can tell you. Angela had even mixed up some of the boys' things with ours, and she was dancing around in an enormous pair of baggy shorts that could only have belonged to Laurence Parker. That awful Delilah Jones, who is by far the tallest girl in the class, was struggling into a skimpy little T-shirt that hardly came down to her tummy button. Jane Baxter, who's really tiny, had shorts almost down to her ankles and a huge pair of plimsolls that flopped about like flippers when she tried to walk. And they were all making so much noise you could hardly hear Miss March's whistle.

'Get out here at once,' stormed Miss March from the corridor, and everybody scrambled towards the door.

I was so busy watching the others that I hadn't

even started getting changed myself. I quickly pulled off my skirt and blouse and grabbed the stuff in my locker, dreading the sight of what Angela had selected for me.

The games kit in my locker was all my own. I stared at the clothes, astonished. I checked the name labels and they all said Charlotte Ellis and I was baffled. Why hadn't Angela mixed up my things as well? I very soon found out.

Miss March was stamping her feet and blowing her whistle like mad by now and everybody had given up trying to sort out the mess and was tumbling out into the corridor. And it was even funnier out there because the boys all started to hoot with laughter when they saw the girls and the girls all screamed and giggled when they caight sight of the boys and the noise was unbelievable.

Laurence Parker was the funniest. He had struggled into the tiniest pair of shorts you ever saw and his big fat belly was sticking out at the top. He had ripped the T-shirt when putting it on and it hung in tatters from his shoulders like the Incredible Hulk's.

'SILENCE!' roared Miss March suddenly, and everybody went quiet.

'Form two lines,' she snapped, and everybody shuffled into place, the boys down one side of the corridor and the girls' line behind Nicola Daley, who had one toe in a very small plimsoll and the other foot in one that looked as if it would fit my dad.

There was a long silence while Miss March glared at us all. All you could hear was her snorting like a dragon. I expected sparks to come flying out of her nose at any minute.

Then she started walking down between the lines, inspecting everybody like a sergeant major in the army, and you could see people's knees tremble as she stopped at each one.

Finally she reached me. She looked me up and down in silence and then suddenly she grabbed me by the shoulder and peered at the name tags in the back of my T-shirt and shorts. Her mouth went into a grim line and that's when it hit me like a ton of bricks. I was the only person in the whole class wearing my own things. My dear friend Angela had done it again.

'That wasn't very clever of you, Charlotte Ellis,' grated Miss March through teeth like tombstones. 'It's perfectly clear who is responsible for this . . . this . . . *riot* this afternoon. You will all change back into your ordinary clothes at once, and we will have a free activities afternoon instead of games.' She looked at me as if I was the nastiest little creature she had ever set eyes on.

'Charlotte Ellis will stay here and sort out this mess. She will put everybody's things exactly where she found them. And there will be no more games for Miss Ellis for the rest of the term.'

My face went scarlet. I could see Angela grinning like a shark at the front of the line. I felt like punching her right in the nose, I can tell you.

'Please, Miss March,' I said quickly. 'It wasn't me. It was . . . it was. . . .'

'Well?' said Miss March, folding her arms and waiting.

But I closed my mouth tight and tears pricked the back of my eyelids. I found I couldn't tell tales, even on somebody as horrible as Angela. I suppose I'm stupid, but that's the way it is.

So everybody else had a lovely afternoon, reading library books, drawing and painting, and working at hobbies like sewing and knitting and weaving and stuff. And I spent the rest of the day sorting out all the games kit. It was an awful job and it took me hours. Only one thing kept me going while I worked. I would walk home with my nice new friend Nicola Daley and tell that Angela Mitchell to go and jump in the river.

Things never work out the way you want them to. When the bell finally went I put the last pair of plimsolls thankfully into the right locker and went for my coat. And there was Nicola coming out of the cloakroom, chatting and smiling away, arm in arm with Angela.

'Walk home with us, Charlie?' invited Angela

cheerfully, offering her other arm as if nothing had happened.

'I'd rather walk home with a crocodile,' I snapped. I meant it, too, At least with a crocodile you always know whose side it's on.

Boffy and the Teacher Eater

Margaret Stuart Barry

Boffy was six years old. He was small and rather thin. Large spectacles covered his pale, serious face. Boffy did not think about tadpoles and chewing-gum and model cars the way other boys did, he wanted more than anything to be an inventor.

'You can't be one until you're grown-up,' said his tall important-looking father. 'You're not old enough.'

'But I'm a genius,' pointed out Boffy.

'Yes,' said his mother, whose name was Mrs Smith, 'I'm afraid he is.'

She found living with a genius very difficult; geniuses are inclined to think it's tea-time when it's only breakfast-time. And they make complicated arrangements with the biscuits instead of just eating them. And *always* use a long word where a short one would do.

Mr Smith was going to work. He was rushing to

31

catch the underground train. Boffy had made a wonderful vehicle out of empty fruit cans. It hopped on and off pavements, knew where not to bump into lamp-posts without being told, and could even climb over things if necessary, like a caterpillar.

'Borrow it,' suggested Boffy. 'It will get you there more quickly.'

'No, thank you,' said Mr Smith politely. He preferred the more conventional form of transport.

So Boffy climbed into the fruit-can vehicle himself, and rattled off to town to collect his mother's groceries. He loaded beans into one container, potatoes into another, and secured half a boiled pig to the back. He took longer doing this than he had expected, so when he came to the gasworks he drove straight over it instead of going round it, which saved a lot of time. This greatly surprised Constable Scuffer. But by the time he'd thought what to do about it Boffy was out of sight.

Mrs Smith was glad to have her groceries so quickly. She wanted to get lunch in the oven early so that she could make a start with her spring-cleaning.

Soon the kitchen was full of buckets and mops and soap and polish and dusters and dishcloths.

'Did you ever see such dust!' she exclaimed. She was red in the face and quite bothered.

'I'll help you,' said Boffy.

'No, thank you,' panted Mrs Smith; she was aghast at the thought of another of Boffy's inventions.

'There must be quicker ways of cleaning a room than this!' Boffy waved his hand at the conglomeration of mops and dusters.

'There is no better way than by getting down on one's hands and knees,' answered his mother, beginning to do just that.

But Boffy was already in his little workshop behind the cabbage patch. He knew exactly what he was going to do because, as I have told you before, he was a genius. In no time at all he had made a large interesting-looking machine. It had a horn at one end, and a plastic sack at the other, and it was held together by a great many rubber tubes.

'What is it?' asked Mrs Smith, as Boffy appeared in the kitchen doorway with the new invention.

'It's a Dust Extractor, of course.'

'Well, I don't need it.' His mother was quite firm. 'I've been doing my spring-cleaning this way for a good many years now, and I don't intend to change.'

'Yes, but look how long it takes you.' Before Mrs Smith could stop him, he had switched on the Dust Extractor.

'It works!' cheered Boffy.

I cannot describe the noise that followed – like a percussion band, but noisier! Anyway, it drowned Mrs Smith's screams of 'Stop! Stop!'

Brooms and mops rattled up into the Dust Extractor. A jar of marmalade flew off the table, followed by cups and saucers and the tablecloth. Boffy was delighted. Not *all* his inventions worked. This one was doing fine. He moved it closer to the cooker, which looked extremely dusty. At once the pans came to life. Off flew the lids and out popped the potatoes and the runner beans. They slithered and bumped down the

tubes of the Dust Extractor. They took the boiling water with them and carried on cooking merrily inside the plastic bag. Last of all the oven door swung open and out shot half a pig.

Mrs Smith was completely DISTRAUGHT.

'You are a DISGRACE!' thundered Boffy's father when he came home for lunch (which was now only a buttered biscuit and a cup of tea). 'You will go straight to your room, without lunch, without afternoon tea, and without supper, and you will *stay* there. And while you are there you will rid your head of all nonsensical ideas.'

'I'm sorry, Father,' apologized Boffy. And he polished his spectacles on his shirt.

It was hard being so awfully clever.

For a whole week Boffy behaved like a model boy – more or less. He sat in the garden and counted bees. When he had counted five hundred and sixty-nine he thought of a number and divided them by it. Then he counted earwigs and subtracted them from the number of leaves on the mulberry bush.

When the dustbin-lorry arrived he carted his Dust Extractor round to the front garden and offered it to the dustbin-men. At first they did not want to take it, but when they saw how it operated they said, 'Thank you very much. This will make our job a whole lot easier.'

And they took it away.

Mr and Mrs Smith didn't know themselves, it was so quiet around the place. Mrs Smith was worried.

'Do you think you ought to have been *quite* so severe with Boffy?' she wondered.

'Well, perhaps not,' answered her husband. 'But we can't have these frightful inventions of his upsetting the whole household.' (He was a little worried himself.)

'If he could invent something small – like a Boiled-egg Opener or a . . . or a. . . .' But Mrs Smith hadn't any more ideas.

'I'll speak to him,' decided Mr Smith quite kindly. 'Boffy,' he shouted down the garden, 'just be more careful in future, that's all.'

'Yes, Father,' answered Boffy. He was relieved.

The following day was a school day. Boffy was in Class IV – on account of his being so clever, that is. He should have been in Class I, but the teacher in that room couldn't cope with him. He was constantly correcting her, and she didn't like that at all. Mr Grim, however, had been to university, so he knew one or two things Boffy didn't.

Today he was in a bad mood, because it was the first day back after a holiday. He stared at the class ferociously and made Jenny Jenny cry. He threw a new piece of chalk at Herbert Entwhistle, and made them all write lines.

'He's horrible, HORRIBLE,' wept Jenny Jenny.

'Don't cry, Jenny Jenny,' comforted Boffy. 'I have an idea. Tomorrow you will have nothing to worry about.'

After tea he retired to his shed behind the cabbage patch and he thought, and he banged and he screwed and he fixed. Then he locked up, kissed his parents good night, and went to bed early. His small head was quite worn out.

Next morning Boffy collected his new invention from the shed and set off to school. He carried it a long way round down the back streets, just in case he should meet any of his important-looking father's important-looking friends. But he met the milkman, and Mr Leggit, the postman, and that was all.

The school cloakroom was packed with children when Boffy appeared in the doorway with his latest invention.

'Oooh, what's that?' asked the children, gathering round.

'It's a Teacher Eater,' explained Boffy.

'Do you mean it actually *eats* teachers?' asked the incredulous children.

'Of course it does,' replied Boffy. 'That's what I've just told you.'

The Teacher Eater was very large. It was a cross between a robot and a dragon. It was constructed chiefly of tin and had a huge jagged

jaw like the blade of a saw. On its face, which was simply enormous, Boffy had painted a big pleasant smile. This was not strictly necessary to the functioning of the machine, but Boffy did not want to frighten Jenny Jenny. He had even troubled to glue a black wig on to the Teacher Eater's head.

'Oooh, I like him!' said Jenny Jenny. 'He's *super*, Boffy!'

Boffy kept the Teacher Eater hidden under a pile of coats until after play, and then he wheeled it out into Class I. The Teacher Eater trundled across the classroom floor and completely devoured the Infants' teacher.

'Hurray!' cheered the children.

The uproar brought the other teachers racing out of their rooms. They clapped their hands and shouted angry commands. The Teacher Eater didn't like that; it trundled more quickly towards them. A crowd of children skipped and jumped behind it. Suddenly it fancied the Art teacher. She was a delectable mouthful. Her scarlet stockings were the last the children saw of her.

'*Mon dieu!*' gasped the French master. He had no time to say any more.

The terrible machine rolled down the corridor hungry for more. It found the Mathematics teacher rather difficult to digest: numbers and question marks shot out of its ears all over the place.

The Teacher Eater was thoroughly enjoying eating teachers. It charged hither and thither gulping them down whole until at last there was not a single one left.

Boffy stored his invention in the games cupboard and locked the door.

'Well, children,' commanded Boffy, 'back to your classrooms, and I shall be round presently.'

No one contradicted. They did as they were told. They were quite content to look upon Boffy as their new Headmaster.

Boffy retired to the Headmaster's room to draw up a new timetable. It consisted chiefly of games and do-as-you-like lessons. The children played games until they were exhausted. In the do-as-you-like lessons most of them went home.

It was not long before every parent was frantically phoning every other parent. The whole town was ringing and buzzing. Mr and Mrs Smith were thoroughly alarmed and more than a little annoyed with their son.

'You are a DISGRACE!' (again) thundered Mr Smith, 'and you will go straight to your room, without tea, without supper, and without breakfast, and you will *stay* there. And whilst you are there you will consider the damage you have done.'

The school governors sat up very late that night discussing hard and partaking of refreshments.

They were very annoyed indeed. The sort of problems they were used to dealing with were problems like whether to buy a heated fish tank, or whether to buy new desks for the Infants. They had never had to deal with a problem like the Teacher Eater. It was all extremely irritating. They decided to visit the school at nine o'clock sharp the following morning. Five minutes later they decided that they wouldn't, as the machine which ate teachers might very well turn out to be a School Governor Eater too!

'Highly probable,' they muttered wisely.

The next day all the children were in school very early. They wanted to see what Boffy had in store for them. They expected that the morning would be spent in playing games, and the afternoon in painting or in general messing around. But Boffy had been considering the matter. He was enjoying being a Headmaster, and he had decided that his pupils should get down to some serious work. He pinned up a large notice in the hall. It read:

1st lesson –   Maths
2nd lesson –   Greek
3rd lesson –   Chemistry
4th lesson –   Lecture in the assembly hall on
                'The Origin of the Species',
                given by Boffy:
                    (signed) Boffy (*Headmaster*)

'What about play-time?' complained Simon Goodbody halfway through the morning.

'You had enough play yesterday,' scolded Boffy sternly.

'But *you're* not working,' persisted Simon sulkily. 'You're just sitting in the Headmaster's room doing nothing.'

'Of course. That's what Headmasters *do*. You will stay in after school and write "I must not be bold" one hundred times.'

Simon hated that. But Boffy sounded so much like a real Headmaster that he was afraid to disobey.

Then a CATASTROPHE happened . . . the Dinner Lady did not appear. She had heard all about the dreadful Teacher Eater and was terrified out of her wits. She was afraid it might turn nasty and become a Dinner Lady Eater too. And so the children had no dinner. Jenny Jenny began to cry.

'I'm hungry, Boffy,' she wailed. 'Ever so hungry.'

'So am I,' said Johnny and Kate the twins. And they began to cry also.

Soon the whole school was wailing and moaning.

'And your lessons are too hard,' gulped Jenny Jenny, quite heartbroken, 'and I can't do them.'

'Neither can I,' sobbed all the others together.

'I wish our teacher was back,' sniffed Jenny Jenny, 'I wish he *was*.'

Boffy was cross (and worried and a bit sorry).
'One just can't please some folks,' he grunted.

At that moment, the school door opened and in stamped Mr Smith looking specially important.

'Now then! Now then!' he bellowed. 'This nonsense has gone on quite long enough. Where is the Teacher Eater, Boffy?'

Obediently Boffy unlocked the games cupboard, and there was the Teacher Eater, gleaming in the electric light.

'Right,' said Mr Smith, pulling it out. 'Now *I* have brought along an invention. It's not a new one, and it's not a big one, but it works. Your mother lent it to me.'

It was a tin opener. Mr Smith started to use it and cut a large hole in the Teacher Eater's back.

Out rolled the Infants' teacher, then the Art mistress followed closely by the Maths master, the French master, and one or two others, and finally the Headmaster himself. They sat in a heap on the floor, looking very dazed and very crumpled. They could not think where they had been or why. Then they caught sight of the Teacher Eater and remembered. The Headmaster turned very pale indeed, then he said, 'There will be a half-day's holiday today. Good afternoon children.'

When Mr Smith had driven his son home he said, 'You are a DISGRACE! (third time) and you will go straight to your room –'

'– without tea, without supper, and without breakfast,' finished Boffy for him. 'And I will consider the damage I have done, and I will *never* invent anything again – not until I'm grown-up anyway.'

Then Mr Smith laughed very loudly, and Mrs Smith laughed too. And they thought how lucky they were after all to have a genius in the family.

And all the other mothers and fathers in the town thought how lucky *they* were that they hadn't.

Friends and Brothers

Dick King-Smith

'You say that word just once more,' said William to Charlie, 'and I'll hit you.'

Charlie said it.

William hit him.

Charlie then let out a screech and kicked William on the shin, and William bellowed.

William and Charlie's mother came rushing in like a whirlwind, with a face like thunder.

'You two will drive me mad!' she stormed. 'All you do is fight, all day long!'

'William hit me,' said Charlie.

'Why did you hit him, William?'

'Because Charlie keeps on saying the same word. Whatever I say, he says the same word, over and over again. Anyway, he kicked me.'

'Will hit me first,' said Charlie.

'William,' said mother, 'you are not to hit Charlie. He is younger than you and much smaller. The next time you do, I shall hit you.'

'You didn't ought to, Mum,' said William.

'Why not?'

'I'm younger than you and much smaller.'

'Absolutely,' said Charlie.

'There you are!' shouted William madly. 'That's the word! Whatever I say, he just says "Absolutely". He doesn't even know what it means.'

'Absolutely,' said Charlie.

William let out a yell of rage and rushed at his brother with his fists clenched. Charlie dodged behind his mother, who held a furious William at arm's length.

'Now *stop* it, the pair of you!' she said.

'William, you stop attacking Charlie, and Charlie, you stop annoying Will. I cannot stand one more minute of being shut in this house with you two. Get your bikes. We'll go to the Park.'

William stumped off, limping slightly from the kick, and shouting angrily 'It's not fair!'

From behind his mother's back, Charlie's face appeared. Silently he mouthed the word 'Absolutely'.

In the Park, William rode his BMX at top speed. He felt the need to be all by himself, miles from anybody. The roads in the Park were full of steep switchback slopes, and William swooped down them flat out. Like a lot of elder brothers, he felt he had had a raw deal.

Charlie, meanwhile, was trying to see how slowly he could pedal without falling off. He had not long inherited William's old bike and was fascinated by the problems of balance. This was much more fun than a tricycle. Like a lot of younger brothers, he had forgotten all about the recent row, and was singing happily to himself. Then he came to the top of one of the steepest slopes. He grinned, and bent low over the handlebars.

His mother, walking some way behind, saw the small figure disappear from view. A moment later, a dreadful wailing started her running hard.

Halfway down the slope, Charlie lay sprawled in the road, the old bike beside him, one wheel still spinning. His face, she saw when she reached him, was covered in blood. There was a deep cut across his forehead and a set of scratches, gravel-studded, down one cheek.

At that moment William came flying back down the reverse slope and skidded to a halt, wide-eyed with horror at the scene.

'What happened?' he said miserably.

'I don't know. He must have touched the brakes and gone straight over the handlebars. Listen carefully, Will. We must get him to hospital quickly – that cut's going to need stitches. I'm going to carry him to the nearest Park gate, that one over there, and try and stop a

car to give us a lift. Can you wheel both bikes and stick them out of sight in those bushes, and then run and catch me up?'

'Yes, Mum,' said William.

He looked at his brother's face. Charlie was still crying, but quietly now.

'He'll be all right, won't he?' William said.

Twenty-four hours later Charlie, recovered now from the shock of his accident, was jabbering away nineteen to the dozen.

He remembered little of the actual crash, or of his treatment in hospital, the stitching of the cut, and the cleaning-up of his gravelly face. It was very swollen now so that one side of him didn't look like Charlie at all, but his voice was as loud and piercing as ever as he plied his brother with endless questions.

'Did you see me come off, Will?'

'No.'

'I went right over the handlebars, didn't I?'

'Suppose so.'

'How fast d'you think I was going, Will?'

'I don't know.'

'A hundred miles an hour, d'you think?' squeaked Charlie excitedly.

'I expect so, Charles,' said William in a kindly voice. 'You looked an awful mess when I got there.'

'Lots of blood, Will?'

'Yes. Ugh, it was horrible.'

'Then what happened?'

'Well, Mum ran all the way to the nearest gate carrying you, and a kind lady in a car stopped and gave us all a lift to the hospital.'

'And then they stitched me up!' said Charlie proudly.

'Yes.'

'Did you see them stitching me up, Will?'

'No, Charles.'

'I expect it was a huge great needle,' said Charlie happily. 'You've never had six stitches, have you, Will?'

'No,' said William. 'You were jolly brave, Charlie,' he said. 'You can have a go on my BMX when you're better.'

'I can't reach the pedals,' Charlie said.

'Oh. Well, you can take a picture with my Instamatic if you like.'

'Can I really, Will?'

'And you can borrow my Swiss Army knife for a bit.'

'Can I really?'

'Yes,' said William. He put his hand in his pocket and pulled out a rather squidgy-looking bar of chocolate.

'And you can have half of this,' he said.

'Gosh, thanks, Will!'

William and Charlie's mother put her head round the door, wondering at the unaccustomed silence, and saw her sons sitting side by side on Charlie's bed, chewing chocolate. William actually had his arm round Charlie's shoulders.

'Look what I've got, Mum,' said Charlie with his mouth full.

'Did you give him some of yours, Will?' said his mother.

'Naturally,' said William loftily. 'We're friends and brothers.'

Another day went by, and Charlie was definitely better. His face was much less swollen, his spirits high, his voice shriller yet.

He had made up a song about his exploits, which he sang, endlessly and very loudly.

'Who came rushing down the hill?
Charlie boy!
Who had such an awful spill?
Charlie boy!
Who came down with a terrible thud,
Covered in mud and covered in blood?
Charlie, Charlie, Charlie boy!'

William, as he occasionally did, had an attack of earache, painful enough without Charlie's singing.

'Charles,' he said as the friend and brother was

just about to come rushing down the hill for the twentieth time, 'd'you think you could keep a bit quiet?'

'Why?' shouted Charlie at the top of his voice.

'Because I've got earache.'

'Oh,' said Charlie in a whisper. 'Oh, sorry, Will. Does it hurt a lot?'

'Yes,' said William, white-faced, 'it does.'

For the rest of the day Charlie tiptoed about the house, occasionally asking William if he needed anything, and, if he did, fetching it. He guarded his brother's peace and quiet fiercely, frowning angrily at his mother when she dropped a saucepan on the kitchen floor.

'Hullo, Charlie boy!' shouted his father on his return from work, 'How's the poor old face?'

'Don't make such a noise, Dad!' hissed Charlie furiously. 'Will's got earache.'

It was now a week since Charlie's accident, a week of harmony and brotherly love.

Charlie's face was now miles better and William's earache quite gone.

They were drawing pictures, at the kitchen table, with felt pens.

'Charles,' said William. 'Can I borrow your red? Mine's run out.'

'No,' said Charlie.

'Why not? You're not using it.'

'Yes, I am,' said Charlie, picking up his red felt and colouring with it.

'You just did that to be annoying,' said William angrily.

The word 'annoying' rang a bell with Charlie, and he grinned and nodded and said 'Absolutely!'

'Charlie!' said William between his teeth. 'Don't start that again or I'll hit you!'

'You can't,' said Charlie. 'I've got a bad face.'

'I'll hit you all the same,' said William.

'I'll shout in your bad ear,' said Charlie, 'and d'you know what I'll shout?'

'What?'

'ABSOLUTELY!!' yelled Charlie and scuttled out of the room with William in hot pursuit, as life returned to normal.

Cheese, Peas and Chocolate Pudding

Betty Van Witsen

There was once a little boy who ate cheese, peas and chocolate pudding. Cheese, peas and chocolate pudding. Cheese, peas and chocolate pudding. Every day the same old things: cheese, peas and chocolate pudding.

For breakfast he would have some cheese. Any kind. Cream cheese, American cheese, Swiss cheese, Dutch cheese, Italian cheese, blue cheese, green cheese, yellow cheese, brick cheese. Just cheese for breakfast.

For lunch he ate peas. Green or yellow peas. Frozen peas, canned peas, dried peas, split peas, black-eyed peas. No potatoes, though – just peas for lunch.

And for supper he would have cheese and peas. And chocolate pudding. Cheese, peas and chocolate pudding. Cheese, peas and chocolate pudding. Every day the same old things: cheese, peas and chocolate pudding.

Once his mother bought a lamb chop for him. She cooked it in a little frying pan on the stove, and she put some salt on it, and gave it to the little boy on a little blue dish. The boy looked at it. He smelled it. (It did smell delicious!) He even touched it. But . . .

'Is this cheese?' he asked.

'It's a lamb chop, darling,' said his mother.

The boy shook his head. 'Cheese!' he said. So his mother ate the lamb chop herself, and the boy had some cottage cheese.

One day his big brother was chewing a raw carrot. It sounded so good, the little boy reached his hand out for a bite.

'Sure!' said his brother. 'Here!' The little boy

almost put the carrot in his mouth, but at the last minute he remembered, and he said, 'Is this peas?'

'No, fella, it's a carrot,' said his brother.

'Peas,' said the little boy firmly, handing the carrot back.

Once his daddy was eating a big dish of raspberry jelly. It looked so shiny red and cool, the little boy came over and held his mouth open.

'Want a taste?' asked his daddy. The little boy looked and looked at the jelly. He almost looked it off the dish. But: 'Is it chocolate pudding?' he asked.

'No, son, it's jelly,' said his daddy.

So the little boy frowned and backed away. 'Chocolate pudding!' he said.

His grandma baked cookies for him. 'Nope!' said the boy.

His grandpa bought him an ice cream cone. The little boy just shook his head.

His aunt and uncle invited him for a fried-chicken dinner. Everybody ate fried chicken and more fried chicken. Except the little boy. And you know what he ate.

Cheese, peas and chocolate pudding. Cheese, peas and chocolate pudding. Every day the same old things: cheese, peas and chocolate pudding.

But one day – ah, one day, a very funny thing

happened. The little boy was playing puppy. He lay on the floor and growled and barked and rolled over. He crept to the table where his big brother was having lunch.

'Arf-arf!' he barked.

'Good doggie!' said his brother, patting his head. The little boy lay down on his back on the floor and barked again.

But at that minute, his big brother dropped a piece of *something* from his plate. And the little boy's mouth was just ready to say 'Arf!' And what do you think happened?

Something dropped into the little boy's mouth. He sat up in surprise. Because *something* was on his tongue. And *something* was warm and juicy and delicious!

And it didn't taste like cheese. And it did *not* taste like peas. And it certainly wasn't chocolate pudding.

The little boy chewed slowly. Each chew tasted better than the last. He swallowed *something* and opened his mouth again. Wide. As wide as he could.

'Want some more?' asked his brother.

The little boy closed his mouth and thought. 'That's not cheese,' he said.

'No, it's not,' said his brother.

'And it isn't peas.'

'No, not peas,' said his brother.

'And it couldn't be chocolate pudding.'

'No, it certainly is not chocolate pudding,' smiled his brother. 'It's hamburger.'

The little boy thought hard. 'I like hamburger,' he said.

So his big brother shared the rest of his hamburger with the little boy, and ever after that, guess what!

Ever after that, the little boy ate cheese, peas, and chocolate pudding and hamburger.

Until he was your age, of course. When he was your age, he ate everything.

The Tidying Up of Thomas

Charlotte Hough

Are you a rough, untidy child? I hope not. I expect you are very neat and clean and careful but, well, anyway, whatever you are you just couldn't be as bad as Thomas was because he was worse than any other boy in the whole of England. It was such a pity, because he was really very lucky. Neat clean careful people like you could have done with some of his toys, and those poor toys could have done with you! Thomas had a great many kind uncles and aunts with no children and plenty of money. They had given him a Noah's ark and a farm and a zoo and soldiers and cars and games and paints and books and goldfish and a rocking-horse and a blackboard and a Red Indian costume and – oh, everything you have ever wanted. And he had a lovely big nursery to keep them all in, with a shiny green floor.

But he was so *rough*, and so *untidy*!

His poor mother was distracted. She didn't know what to do about Thomas.

One day he fetched the scissors out of her workbox and tried to take out his big bear's appendix. He pulled out all the stuffing and made such a mess of him that poor old Teddy would have had to be *thrown away* if Thomas's mother hadn't relented and collected it all up with a dustpan and brush and sewn him up again.

'You're a very naughty, wasteful, silly little boy!' she scolded him, 'and you don't deserve all those lovely toys. Tomorrow you shan't play in the nursery at all!'

So the next day Thomas had to play in the kitchen while his mother was writing letters, and when she went in to make the tea she found he had mixed up the sugar and the flour and the barley and the tea and he had broken the coffee-pot and spilt the vinegar. 'Oh, Thomas, Thomas!' she cried, 'I only hope you're ashamed of yourself!'

But Thomas wasn't ashamed of himself, not in the least bit! He thought he was really very clever.

He put the blackboard chalks in the pencil sharpener and made coloured powder and used it for gunpowder to make indoor fireworks with, but that didn't go right, so he left all the firework things in a heap on the floor and scribbled on the faces of the people in his books. He took the tyres off the cars and mixed them all up with the

cowboys and Indians, and oh, so many naughty things you would hardly believe it. Not things that you would *ever* do!

Of course somebody as naughty as Thomas never goes to bed without making a terrible fuss and to-do about it. First he would refuse to go at all, and after his bath he always had to be sent back to the bathroom because he hadn't washed his ears, and then back again because he hadn't cleaned out the bath. He had always either broken his comb or lost his toothbrush or torn his pyjamas. By the time he was really and truly in bed and asleep his parents felt absolutely exhausted.

'We shall really have to do something about that boy,' said Thomas's father.

'Oh yes, I quite agree, we shall really *have* to,' said his mother, 'but what? We've tried smacking him, and stopping his sweets, and reasoning with him, and . . . and praising him when he's good, only he's never good, so *that* didn't work. We've tried everything.'

Meanwhile in the darkened nursery all the toys were waking up and cautiously feeling their bruises and sorting themselves out. What a rustling and whispering there was! The farmer was collecting up his flock of sheep from amongst the bricks, while Mr Noah and the zoo-keeper tried to track down *their* animals, and a toy soldier climbed stiffly out of the goldfish bowl, shaking the water out of his busby. A squeaky trumpeting came from under the bookcase, where the little zoo elephant had got pinned under a battered police-car. Luckily his friend the woolly elephant was able to pull him free and help him back to the broken cardboard box which was shared by the zoo with various paperclips, lumps of plasticine and other odds and ends.

'We shall really have to do something about that boy,' said the kangaroo, as she searched for her baby amongst the dressing-up clothes (she eventually found him in the paintbox).

'Oh yes, I quite agree, we really *have* to,' said the woolly snake, 'but what? I can't do much to help. I've completely lost one eye and my head's getting all loose because he always picks me up by it though I distinctly heard them telling him not to.'

'You're lucky,' said a tin bus bitterly. 'Do you know, he used me instead of a hammer the other day? I've hardly got any paint left and I used to be such a beautiful red.'

'Well, look at me,' put in the rocking-horse. 'It's shocking, it really is. No mane, no tail, no stirrups, no nothing. Wobbling-horse would be a better name for me now after all my rough treatment. I'm really getting quite dangerous.'

At this the others all nodded their heads very gravely. No toy likes to be called dangerous: it is a dreadful thing for a toy to be. But it was true that the rocking-horse's bolts were getting worn and bent and it was already quite difficult to stick on him without falling off, at a gallop. Everyone knew what happened to dangerous toys: they were thrown away just as soon as anybody suspected it, before you could say 'Dustbin!' and that was the end of them. Mr Noah glanced anxiously up at the roof of the ark, which had been wrenched half off, leaving a nail showing, and the tin bus felt the jagged bit that had been left last time Thomas had thrown him at the cat, and hit the fireplace instead.

There was a thoughtful silence, broken only by a sneeze every now and then as the poor toys breathed in the dust. For a long time the nursery had been in such a mess that it was quite impossible for anybody to clean it properly.

'Well,' said the rocking-horse at last, raising his head determinedly, 'I don't like being unkind but we really can't go on like this. There is nothing else for it. We shall have to give him back some of his own medicine.'

In the middle of the night Thomas woke up. Something was scratching him. 'Bother!' he said. 'I must have left something in my bed!' and he ferreted about and found a small tin turkey. 'That's funny!' he said, 'I don't remember playing with that up here!' And he threw it out and closed his eyes.

But Thomas couldn't go to sleep. However much he rolled over in bed he always managed to lie on something hard and spiky. In the end he got up, switched the light on, and pulled his bed to pieces. There amongst the bedclothes lay all the farm animals with their sharp little legs. There were pigs in the pillowcase, sheep in the sheets, cows in the coverlet, bulls in the blankets and hens and ducks and milking girls *everywhere*

Thomas shook them angrily out on to the floor and then he tried to make his bed again.

Thomas wasn't good at making beds. He had an uncomfortable night.

At half past seven he was up and dressed, without anybody even calling him once, pleased to leave that horrid, cold, and lumpy heap of bedclothes. He started to get his things ready for school before breakfast so that there wouldn't be the usual awful rush. (As you know, untidy children are always in an awful rush because they never know where anything is. That's why it's *so* much better to be like you.)

Before long he went running into the kitchen to find his mother. 'Look at my nature book!' he cried indignantly, holding it up before her eyes.

'Well, it's a nasty messy-looking thing,' agreed

his mother. 'But so are all your other books.'

'But this is a *school* book!' cried Thomas. 'You can't scribble on *school* books. We aren't allowed to!'

His mother looked at it more closely. 'But you have done, dear,' she said mildly. 'With all your coloured chalks.'

'But it wasn't me that did it!' shouted Thomas, nearly in tears.

'Now, Thomas,' said his mother, putting down the milk-jug and turning to face him, 'I know you're a rough, untidy boy but at least you always used to be a truthful one. I didn't scribble on your book and neither did your father. That only leaves one person who could have, doesn't it? Now, sit down and eat your breakfast and don't let me ever hear you speak an untruth again!'

Thomas opened his mouth, and then he looked at his mother's face, which was rather unusually firm, so he changed his mind and shut it again. Silently he ate his breakfast and silently he went upstairs to the bathroom to clean his teeth.

Silently he gazed at the row of empty toothpaste tubes. Silently he fetched a bowl and a cloth and cleaned the toothpaste off the bath, the floor, the walls, the door. Somebody had been enjoying themselves. Thomas worked hard. He had a wholesome respect for his father, who seldom visited the nursery, but was shortly expected in

the bathroom in order to shave.

Ten minutes later, Thomas rushed madly into the hall to get ready for school and a moment later another loud wail reached his mother's ears. 'I can't wear *this*!'

'What's the matter now, dear?'

'There aren't any buttons on my blazer!'

'Nonsense dear, they can't all have gone, not all at once!'

'They have! Just look!'

'Good gracious! So they have!' said his mother in astonishment. 'Whatever made you do such a thing? You've cut them all off! Well, there's no time to sew them on again now. You'll just have to go as you are. Really, Thomas, I can't think what's got into you! I'll just have to hide all the scissors in the house. Every single pair. You don't seem to have any *sense*!'

'But listen!' cried Thomas desperately. 'I . . . didn't . . . do . . . it!'

'Thomas! remember what I said,' warned his mother. 'Untidiness is one thing. Untruth is another.'

'But don't you see? THE TOYS DID IT!'

'Well, dear, if the toys did it I can't say I blame them, seeing the way you treat them. Perhaps now you'll realize what it's like, being treated that way. Perhaps it will teach you a lesson!'

And do you know, it did! It was really quite amazing – everybody remarked on it. 'What a lovely nursery!' they say now when they come to tea with Thomas. 'It's so neat and clean and tidy, with everything all ready for playing with, in its proper place! How nice it is to see somebody who really appreciates his toys!' and they wish that *their* little boy or girl was as good!

It's an extra special nursery.

Some people even say the toys have extra special expressions on their faces, but that seems to be going a bit far, really, don't you think?

The Not-Very-Nice-Prince

Pamela Oldfield

Prince Ferdinand was not very nice and hardly anybody liked him. Only the Princess Eglantine could put up with his rude manners, and they would visit each other fom time to time for a game of Snakes and Ladders.

One day the Prince was driving home in the royal coach when it came to a sudden halt. An old woman was crossing the road with an ancient pram laden with firewood.

The Prince put his head out of the window and shouted at her. 'I say, old woman, move that flipping pram out of my way and look sharp about it.'

The old woman looked at him. She was very ugly indeed and in need of a good wash.

'Hang on a minute, your Highness,' she croaked. 'This nearside wheel's a bit wobbly. . . .'

Now a gentleman would have offered to help her but Prince Ferdinand was no gentleman.

70

'Don't bother me with your excuses,' he
shouted. 'Get the flipping thing out of my way.'

Well, the ugly old woman was really a witch.
She didn't like his manners and decided to teach
him a lesson. She pointed at him with a long bony
finger and muttered some magic words. He heard
the word 'flipping' but that was all.

At once the 'flipping thing' flipped. To
Ferdinand's dismay the pram rose into the air
and turned right over. All the firewood fell out on
to the startled horses.

They were very frightened and promptly ran

away and the coach came unhitched and rolled into the hedge. The Prince climbed out of his wrecked coach and looked for the old woman but she had disappeared. He didn't know that she had put a spell on him.

But the next day a girl came to the door with a basket of eggs.

'Good day to your Highness,' she said politely. 'Will you buy some new-laid eggs?'

'No, I won't,' he said without even a thank you.

'But they are beautiful brown eggs,' she said.

'They may be sky-blue pink for all I care,' he said. 'Take the flipping things away.'

You can guess what happened!

The basket rose up into the air and turned over. The eggs fell on the Prince's best velvet coat and ruined it.

'Now I see it all!' he cried fearfully. 'The old woman was a witch and she has put a spell on me. I shall have to be very careful what I say from now on.'

The Not-Very-Nice-Prince walked about all next day with his hand clapped over his mouth so that he wouldn't say anything foolish . . . but the next morning he forgot again. When the maid carried in his breakfast he sat up in bed and scowled.

'What on earth is that?' he asked.

'Crunchy Pops, your Highness.'

'Crunchy Pops!' he grumbled. 'I wanted eggs

and bacon. Take the flipping things – Ooh!'

Too late he realized what he'd said. The bowl of Crunchy Pops floated into the air and flipped right over. It emptied itself all over his head. Prince Ferdinand screamed with rage and the terrified maid fled into a nearby broom cupboard and wept copiously.

After that, things went from bad to worse. The Prince became very flustered and that made him even more forgetful. On Monday he flipped a royal banquet.

On Tuesday it was a market stall.

On Wednesday it was a troop of the King's best soldiers!

But he had finally gone too far.

'Get out of my sight,' roared the King, stamping his foot so hard that it hurt.

'Don't come back until the spell is lifted.'

Notices were put up warning people to keep away from the Prince and they didn't need telling twice.

So the unfortunate Ferdinand retired to a dark dungeon below the palace and wondered what he should do. He didn't tell anyone where he was and no one bothered to find out – which was very sad.

One day the Princess Eglantine visited the King for a game of croquet. She had almost won the game when she caught sight of the Prince watching them from the dungeon. Kindly, she offered to visit him for a game of Snakes and Ladders.

'How can I concentrate on Snakes and Ladders at a time like this?' he wailed. 'All I need is a flipping Princess who—'

He had done it again! Slowly the Princess rose into the air and turned over.

She came down on her bottom and everyone laughed.

The Princess was mortified. 'I shall be back when the spell is lifted and *not* before,' she told the King, and stomped off home with her nose in the air.

The question was – who could lift the spell? The only visitor to the dark dungeon was an old woman who took him bread and water each day. Prince Ferdinand was so busy feeling sorry for himself he didn't even recognize her. He had plenty of time to ponder his manners and vowed that if the spell were ever lifted he would be a reformed character.

One day the old woman, who was really the witch, came into the dungeon. She had a pail of water and a scrubbing brush and she began to scrub the floor. The Prince looked at her kindly.

'That is hard work for an old woman,' he said politely. 'Please let me help you.'

To the old woman's dismay he seized the scrubbing brush and fell to scrubbing the dungeon floor. She stared at him in horror.

'You nincompoop!' she roared. 'You numb-skull! Why do you have to be so polite? Your cursed good manners have lifted the spell – and broken my power also . . . Aah!'

And she vanished in a puff of horrid green smoke which smelled like burnt kippers.

Of course, the people were delighted. They carried Ferdinand through the streets rejoicing – all the way to the Princess Eglantine's palace. She was waiting eagerly for the Very-Nice-Prince and another game of Snakes and Ladders.

The Arguing Boy

Leila Berg

Now this is a tale of a boy who argued. And this is the way *I* tell it.

Once upon a time there was a boy. And he had nine big sisters. And because there were nine of them and only one of him, he always argued.

One day he had argued so much with his nine big sisters that he decided to seek his fortune. His mammy made him some sandwiches – jam butties, he called them – and she put them in a bag, and he tied them to a pole over his shoulder, which is what people do when they seek their fortune, and off he went.

The weather was terrible. It poured. The rain went straight down his collar, shot down his back, and came out of the bottom of his jeans. And his sandwiches turned into pudding. He walked along, squelch, squelch.

At last he came to a house. He decided to knock

at the door and ask if he could sleep there, in the dry.

'Can I sleep in your house?' he said to the lady.

'I'm afraid you can't.'

'But I'm sopping wet,' he said, starting to argue.

'I know you are, you poor wee thing,' she said. 'But I haven't got room.'

'You've got plenty of room,' he said, arguing. 'You've got a whole house.'

'I'm afraid it's full of people. Tell you what, I'll give you some hot soup to make you feel better. There's plenty of that still cooking.'

'I don't want hot soup. I want to sleep here.' He was very rude.

Just then the lady's husband put his head out of the door. 'Having trouble?' he said. 'Trying to sell you a vacuum cleaner, is he?'

'He wants to sleep here,' said the lady. 'I've told him we haven't got room.'

'I should say we have *not*,' said the man. 'We've a big party here, and people are sleeping everywhere.'

'They can't be *everywhere*. There must be *some* room,' said the boy, arguing away, moving his feet on the doorstep, squelch, squelch.

'There's no room at all,' said the man. 'But I'll tell you what –' And here he started to whisper in the woman's ear.

'Oooh!' said the woman. 'He couldn't!'

'Yes I can!' said the boy. He was just arguing.

Whisper, whisper, went the man. 'Oooh! He'd be scared to death!' said the woman.

'I wouldn't!' said the boy, arguing again.

Whisper, whisper, went the man. And this time the woman said, 'Well, you can tell him. But don't blame me if the Bogey gets him.'

Then the man said to the boy, 'You see, it's like this. We've got a cottage next door.

78

There's nobody in it because of the little Red Bogey.'

'The little Red Bogey? What's that?'

'Oh, he's a sort of hobgoblin. Very fierce and bad-tempered. Perhaps you'd better not go in.'

'I will,' said the boy.

'I thought you would,' said the man. And he gave him the key.

Inside the cottage it was dry, but very dusty. No one had cleaned it for years because of the little Red Bogey.

The boy found a pile of firewood and lit a fire with some matches he found on the shelf. Soon it was blazing away. He took off his boots, spread his clothes on the floor to dry off, and lay down on the bed in the corner.

He was almost asleep in the flickering firelight and the steam coming up from his clothes and boots, when a voice said, 'I am coming!'

He didn't take much notice. After a moment, the voice said again, rather louder, 'I AM COMING!' He still took no notice.

But after another moment the voice fairly bawled, 'I AM COMING!'

He sat up and shouted, 'If you're coming then COME, or else shut up!'

A pile of soot fell down from the chimney. Then two dead birds who had been stuck there good-ness knows how long. Then a lumpy red foot reached down, then a second one, then the rest of the two lumpy legs, then a lumpy, bumpy, frumpy-looking little red man came scrambling down the bricks, and jumped right across the fire into the room.

'Well, what a shrimp!' said the boy. 'The noise you were making, I thought you were a giant at least!'

'Don't you talk to me like that!' said the little man. 'I'm the Red Bogey.'

'I don't care if you're a pink cauliflower,' said the boy.

The little man strode to the door and flung it open. Two men were standing there, one on each side, and they really *were* giants. 'We've got trouble here,' he said. 'Arguing boy. I may be needing you.'

The first one saluted. 'Just give us a call, sir.'

'We'll chop him into pieces,' said the second.

'Right,' said the little Red Bogey. 'Stay there.' And he closed the door again.

'Now are you frightened?' he said to the boy.

'Not a bit,' said the boy.

The little Red Bogey scowled at him, then strode into the kitchen. 'Follow me!' he shouted.

'Why should I?' said the boy.

'You'll be sorry if you don't,' said the little Red Bogey.

'Who says so?' said the boy.

'You'll be sorry if you don't,' said the little Red Bogey, grinding his teeth and swishing his tail, 'because I am going to show you something very interesting indeed, and you will be very sorry if you miss it.'

The boy thought a minute or two, then followed him. 'I *might* come,' he said.

The little Red Bogey pulled open a trap-door in the kitchen floor. Underneath were stairs leading to a cellar. 'Get down there!' he said.

'Why should I?' said the boy.

'You're frightened of the dark, I bet,' said the little Red Bogey.

'I am *not*!' said the boy. And he went down.

At the bottom was an enormous chest.

'Open it!' said the little Red Bogey.

'Open it yourself!' said the boy.

'Oh, you really are a nuisance,' said the little Red Bogey. 'You really make me so tired.' And he started to pull at the lid. He was very small, and the chest was very big, and the lid very heavy by the look of it. But the boy didn't help him at all.

The little Red Bogey kicked the chest, and pulled it, and shouted at the boy, 'You're as bad as I am!'

In the end, after a particularly heavy thump, the lid flew open and there was a pile of golden coins inside, flashing and glittering.

'Here! Who does that belong to?' said the boy.

'It's mine. All mine,' said the little Red Bogey.

'I don't believe you,' said the boy.

'Yes, it is!' shouted the little Red Bogey. 'But I'm giving it to you, if you'll only give me a chance. I'm giving it to you and the people next door.'

'No, you're not,' said the boy. 'Where did you get it?'

'I stole it.'

'Then give it back.'

'I can't give it back. It was hundreds of years ago. I've been trying to give it away over and over again, but everyone runs away from me.'

'Well it's nothing to do with me. I don't want it,' said the boy, and started to go up the steps again.

'It's a rule!' shouted the little Red Bogey. 'I stole it from a human being. So I've got to give it back to a human being. That's the rule!'

The boy stood still and thought, while the little Red Bogey waved his tail like an angry cat.

Then he said, 'Oh well, if there's a rule, that's different. All right, I'll take it.'

'Thank goodness for that,' said the little Red Bogey. 'Let me get away from you and have some peace.' And he dashed up the steps, and the boy came into the room just in time to see the red knobbly feet vanishing up the chimney.

'I wonder if the giants are still outside the door,' he said. But they'd gone too.

In the morning, the man and woman from next door came round to see if he was all right. They were pleased to find him still there, and very surprised to hear about the money. Very pleased too.

The boy bought four tins of paint with some of his share, and painted the cottage yellow and white so that he could live there. Later he asked their daughter to marry him, and when she said no, he argued.

But she said, 'If you argue with me, I'll never speak to you again. Ask me again next year, without arguing in between.'

And the next year she said yes.

They had twelve children, six of them boys, six of them girls. And none of them ever argued, not even about how that chestful of money had got into the cottage in the first place.

Snip snap snover
That story's over

Freddie, the Toothbrush Cheat

Wendy Craig

Freddie sat at the kitchen table collecting crumbs and arranging them in a circle around the rim of his plate. His mother was at the sink, elbow-deep in foam, washing the dishes after supper, and Freddie looked up at her feeling warm and full and sleepy. It would soon be bedtime; Freddie didn't mind going to bed too much in the winter when it was dark and cold outside and he could wriggle down in his bed like a snake with his comics and have a little read and a laugh before the light went out. But then his heart sank; he would have to have a bath and clean his teeth. Ugh.

Now Freddie was a friendly boy, very pleasant company and fun to be with, but he hated soap and water with all his heart and, even more, hated cleaning his teeth. The whole business bored and annoyed him so much that the thought of it made him want to hide from his mother, or even run away rather than have to go through with it again. He felt depressed and stuck his thumb in his mouth and gave it a good suck, at the same time twirling a strand or two of hair with his other hand. His mother had just finished putting away the last knife and fork in the drawer when she saw him from the corner of her eye.

'Come on, Freddie, you look tired, darling. It's half past eight, I'll just go and run your bath.' And she went upstairs.

Freddie let out a groan and felt himself sag. 'Here we go again,' he thought. 'All that palaver. Soap in my eyes, up my nose, in my mouth, and that awful, boring toothbrush.' He could bear it no longer and furtively climbed into the kitchen waste-bin and pulled the lid over himself. It was a bit smelly in there. They'd had kippers for tea and the bones crushed under his shoes, but it was preferable he thought to the smell of rose-pink soap. He heard his mother re-enter the kitchen. She called him, then sighed when he didn't answer. Lifting the flap of the waste-bin an inch or two, he found himself gazing at her flowery apron and he quickly shut it again, but she heard the thud and pulled him out without ceremony and chased him up the stairs whacking his bottom with the loofah.

Freddie was in a frightful rage by now; he shouted and wailed, whilst his mother soaped and scrubbed him. The flannel got in his mouth, and his ears filled with bubbles, hot angry tears dripped into the lather as he slipped and slithered in an attempt to escape his mother's grasp, but she held him firmly and didn't let him escape until he was rosy and clean, and wrapped in a warm white towel.

'Oh, Freddie,' sighed his mother, rubbing his hair dry, 'I'm sick of you being so naughty at bath-time; it really wears me out. You can clean your own teeth, I'm going downstairs to see if Daddy's in yet.'

Freddie sat on the bathroom floor sucking his thumb. He was surrounded by little pools of water and patches of foam, the result of his battle. He hadn't won round one, but he was determined to win round two. He picked up his toothbrush, ran it under the tap, took the top of the tube, spread it here and there as if he'd spat it out in the bottom of the basin, and then got into bed feeling rather pleased with himself. He didn't know why, but he didn't enjoy his comic that night; he couldn't smile once, not even at Korky the Cat, who was usually his favourite.

The next morning, after breakfast, his mother said, 'Go and clean your teeth, Freddie. I don't want to have to start the day with a quarrel, so you can do it by yourself.'

Freddie climbed the stairs with a sly grin. He

put his toothbrush under the tap, made a few splashing and spitting noises, spread a bit of toothpaste around the bottom of the basin and gazed triumphantly at himself in the mirror. He smiled gleefully, but quickly closed his mouth when he noticed that his teeth were pale yellow.

For pudding that day, Mother made a blackberry pie and for supper he finished with chocolate mousse. Freddie was quite good in the bath that night and said he would clean his own teeth. After splashing the toothbrush around for a while he grinned in the mirror and was surprised to see his teeth were brownish-grey with blackberry

seeds stuck between the spaces. He didn't sleep well at all.

The next morning after the same performance had gone on, Freddie bared his teeth in the mirror and found to his dismay that his teeth were pale green, and dotted with blackberry seeds. Still, it was better than the boring business of teeth-cleaning, and he was careful not to smile at anyone that day and only spoke with his hand over his mouth, much to everyone's amazement.

That night he spent ages making teeth-cleaning noises, spitting and sploshing about. He was afraid to look at his teeth which was hardly surprising for now they were quite black and tasted foul – and little did he know, but the blackberry seeds had started to take root.

The next few days were misery; little shoots began to grow around his gums, and tendrils with small leaves kept popping out of his mouth. He had to keep pushing them back in again in case anyone noticed. He was afraid to speak, of course, and just answered his parents with a 'Mmmmm' or a nod. His mother didn't mention his teeth, but he couldn't help feeling he wished she would.

After four weeks of not cleaning his teeth, Freddie was a dreadful sight. His mouth was a tangle of weeds and he was so thin through not eating, and so lonely through not speaking, that his heart was breaking.

His mother, greatly distressed, called the doctor.

His examination was brief. 'This child has not been cleaning his teeth!' he said, shaking his thermometer gravely and trying to part the branches to insert it in his mouth. 'There's nothing I can do for him I'm afraid. He'll have to go to the dentist!'

Freddie's mother was horrified. 'Why, Freddie,' she exclaimed, 'you are a silly boy. You think you have been cheating me but really you've been cheating yourself, and look what it's led to. I've never seen such a ghastly sight in my life. Put on your coat. We're off to the dentist at once.'

The dentist was a jolly chap. 'This is the worst case of non-teeth-cleaning I've ever come up against, my boy,' he said, and set to work with his probes and files and tweezers, disentangling the jungle in Freddie's mouth.

Freddie was half an hour in the dentist's chair and his teeth were given a final polish with a tickly brush whizzing round on the end of the drill. Then the dentist handed him a mirror and said, 'Now smile, Freddie – that's how your teeth should look.'

They were rows of gleaming white pearls set in firm pink gums – a lovely sight. Nobody ever had to tell Freddie to clean his teeth again.

Acknowledgements

The compiler and publishers would like to thank the following for the use of copyright material in this collection:

Curtis Brown Ltd for 'Boffy and the Teacher Eater' by Margaret Stuart Barry from *More Stories for Seven-year Olds* and 'Isabelle the Itch' by Constance C. Green from *Isabelle the Itch*.

Dutton Children's Books, a division of Penguin Books USA Inc for 'Cheese, Peas and Chocolate Pudding' by Betty van Witsen from *Believe and Make Believe* edited by Lucy Sprague Mitchell and Irma Simonton Black. Copyright © 1956 by the Bank Street College of Education, renewed 1984 by the Bank Street College of Education.

Hamish Hamilton Ltd for 'Trouble with the Fiend' by Sheila Lavelle from *Trouble with the Fiend*.

Hatton and Baker Ltd for 'Freddie, the Toothbrush Cheat' by Wendy Craig from *Happy Endings*, published by Hutchinson.

William Heinemann Ltd for 'Friends and Brothers' by Dick King-Smith from *Friends and Brothers* and 'The Tidying up of Thomas' by Charlotte Hough from *Charlotte Hough's Holiday Book*.

Hodder and Stoughton Ltd for 'The Not-very-nice Prince' by Pamela Oldfield from *Helter Skelter*.

Methuen Children's Books for 'The Arguing Boy' by Leila Berg from *Tales for Telling*.

Penguin Books for 'The Boy who made Faces' by Eileen Colwell from *Bad Boys* compiled by Eileen Colwell (Longman Young Books, 1972), © Eileen Colwell 1972.